Experimenting with Science about Yourself

Alan Ward

Illustrated by Zena Flax

CHELSEA JUNIORS
A division of Chelsea House Publishers
New York · Philadelphia

Contents

First Printing

1 3 5 7 9 8 6 4 2

ISBN 0-7910-1512-2

Preface

Nothing is more precious than your own body, nor more wonderful. As a child, you are probably lucky enough to be able to take your body and health for granted – although you do care about other children who are not so fortunate. Adults will tell you that they value fitness and health more than just having a lot of money. All the best pleasures in life come from feeling "great" and enjoying a lively mind. These are the joys of being alive, and of being you.

This book will help you to appreciate and understand the miracle of that incredible acting, sensing and thinking machine which "you" inhabit, like a ghost in a house of marvels. The cleverest people cannot agree about what "you" or "I" are. Many believe that you are more than a body and brain, and that you possess a personal spirit or soul that never dies. Some computer scientists believe that, when their machines can be made more powerful and "clever", they will automatically act as if they were alive. These are exciting, but difficult ideas that might become clearer in your lifetime.

In the meantime, enjoy this little book – for its simple things to do and think about, and for the information it provides. Parents and teachers will find in it many ideas for occupying young children purposefully. Older children can be depended upon to read for pleasure and learning, and – most importantly – to try out the easy-to-do projects. Here is a book that will make you amazed at being alive, but do not be surprised if it inspires you to ask harder questions that will take you to the library, in search of deeper books about being human.

Who are you?

There is nobody quite like you. Remember 5 happy things that happened to you – even quite little things, like being given a favorite comic to read on holiday. Write down these memories. Now put down 5 sad memories. They are parts of being you. Talking about them, if that does not upset you, makes you a person who is interesting to some other person – somebody whose memories are different.

Ask your closest friend to share happy and sad memories. Perhaps you could ask a grandmother or grandfather. You might be able to tape-record this interview. People may be different from each other, but they also agree on many ideas. Make lists of topics which you and another person agree and disagree about.

Would you say that you are a clever person? Everybody is clever sometimes. A brilliant man once said that every single man and woman in a great crowd could do something better than he could – even if it were simply being able to whistle a song in tune, keep a room tidy, quiet a frightened pet, grow flowers, make pebbles skip over the surface of the sea, or be patient with grumpy people. Be honest: What skills make you a special person?

You are a human being – a member of humanity

Through your parents' mothers and fathers (your grandparents), their mothers and fathers (your great-grandparents), and your other ancestors (the people in your family who lived before you), you are related to people who lived long ago. How far back in time can you trace your ancestors? You can draw a chart of your ancestors, called a family tree – and draw and color in a coat of arms, as a badge to represent your family. (You might even discover that your family already has a coat of arms!)

Eric Jones (schoolteacher) — GRANDFATHER
Mary Lewis (artist) — GRANDMOTHER
Cyril Bird (shopkeeper) — GRANDFATHER
Jane Banks (secretary) — GRANDMOTHER

James Jones (engineer) — FATHER
Helen Bird (ambulance driver) — MOTHER

ME

A few million years ago, all the many different colored races of humanity came from similar ancestors. Yes, human beings make up an ancient family with vast numbers of branches and relatives. You are a member of the family. Perhaps your children, or their children, will travel away from Earth, to colonize other planets. You are a part of the future.

In what ways are boys and girls alike? In what ways are they different? Some women are soldiers and some men are cooks. As with young and old and different races, men and women make life richer by expressing their best ways and skills, yet as *people* they are equal.

Your body – and your ideal self

Draw an outline of your body. Then, without looking at a book, draw in the following body parts – putting them where you think they should be: brain, heart, lungs, stomach, intestines (the coiled pipe that your food passes through), kidneys, bladder – any other parts you can think of.

When you have done this, check your drawing with pictures in a biology book. Afterwards you could try the drawing again. It ought to be more accurate than before. Share this game with your friends.

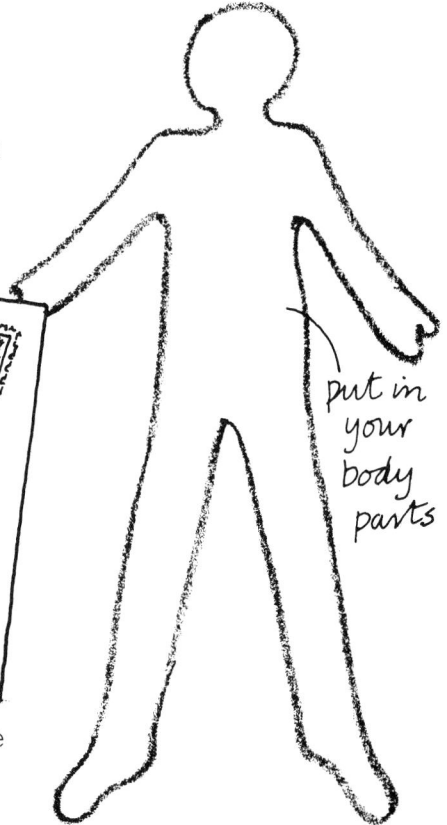

Arthur White
10 Rise Avenue
Smithtown
Johnson County
United States
North America
Northern Hemisphere
Earth
The Solar System
Milky Way Galaxy
THE UNIVERSE

put in your body parts

Draw a picture of the ideal person you wish to be. Be practical: only put in details which would be possible if you tried really hard. Label the drawing to increase the information it shows.

Body and mind

Imagine a speck, smaller than this period. You would need a microscope to see it. Your body is made from millions of such "specks" – they are called cells. In some ways cells are like bricks which go into building a great house, but the cells which make up you are alive. Skin, bone, muscle, blood: all have special sorts of cells. Red blood cells are coin-shaped. Muscle cells are shaped like rods. Nerve cells are round or oval, with spiky points and long threads with endings that look like roots. Bundles of these threads are your nerves. A nerve cell may be tiny, but its invisibly thin nerve thread may be nearly a yard long. Your brain contains ten billion nerve cells – the number being written as 10,000,000,000. Another way to say this number is "ten thousand millions".

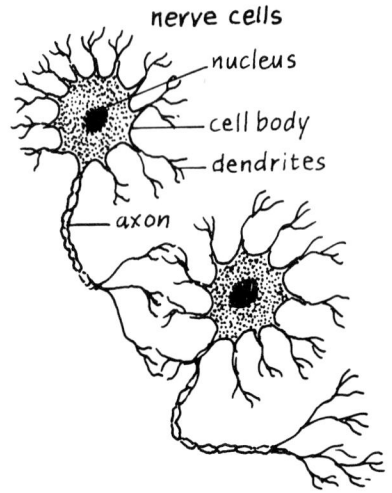

nerve cells
nucleus
cell body
dendrites
axon

Try to imagine ten billion

Start with one million. There are 10,000 *hundreds* in a million. I have just found that a pile of a hundred playing-cards measures 1 in high. 10,000 of these piles, on top of each other, adds up to quite a skyscraper – 300 yards tall in fact!

A million divided by a hundred is ten thousand.

$$\frac{1,000,000}{100} = 10,000$$

that's the hundredth card

the pile is 1 in high

etc!

Ten billion divided by a million is ten thousand.

$$\frac{10,000,000,000}{1,000,000} = 10,000$$

Ten billion playing-cards would make a pile equal in height to 10,000 of these million-card piles. Its height would be immense – almost the same as the distance between Britain and America.

Take time and thought to work out how many miles high that pile of ten billion playing-cards would be. Then you will begin to appreciate the unimaginable number of brain cells you possess. *We will not even mention the unbelievable total of ALL the different cells in your body!*

The brain is your body's main control center

the brain
- skull
- cerebrum
- cerebellum
- spinal cord
- vertebrae

Brain cells are loosely connected by their spiky bits and nerve threads. Electrical signals, called pulses, pass between the cells all the time, even when you are asleep. Pulses are carried to the brain by other nerves leading from parts of your body which sense touch, sight, sound, etc. This tells your mind about the world around. Your mind, acting through the brain, sends pulses out along different nerves, to make your body move. Other pulses control important actions which you do not need to think about, such as heartbeat, breathing and your balance. Many pulses just pass to and fro in your brain, to give you memories, feelings, thoughts and dreams.

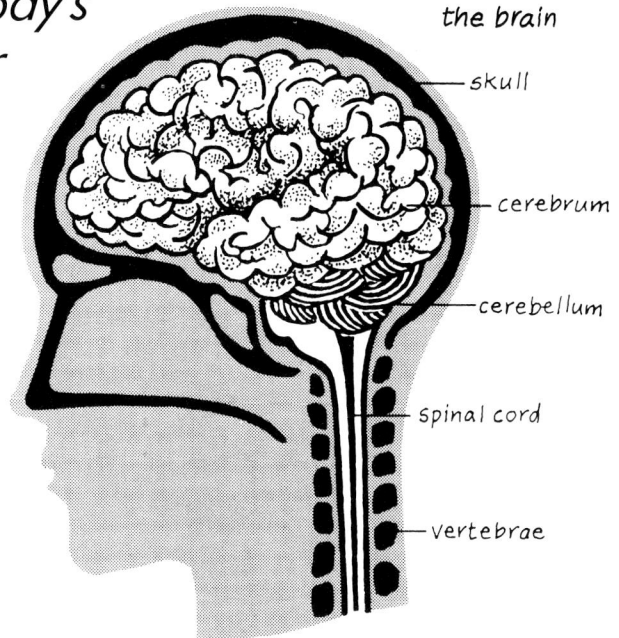

the nervous system

- brain
- spinal cord
- spinal nerves

The greatest number of nerves going to and from the brain are in your spinal cord. This is protected inside the little bones that make your backbone or spine. The brain and nerves of the spinal cord are parts of the *central nervous system*. Nerves and nerve cells outside the brain, but connected with your spinal cord and senses, carry signals that control the ways your glands and other body organs (your stomach and intestines, for example) work together, keeping you lively and fit. Like the brain control of breathing and balancing, these other activities between parts of your body are automatic.

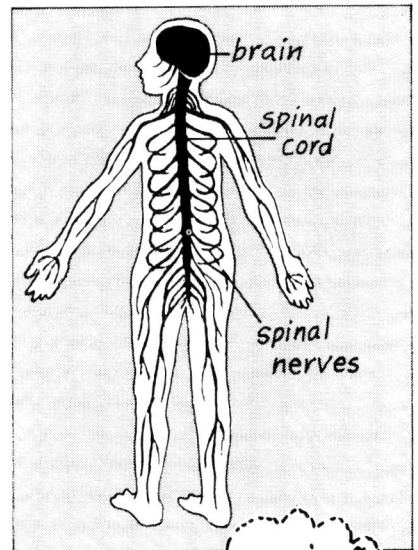

What is your mind?

dreaming

Some people think that a mind is just a brain "knowing about itself". Other people think it is like a ghost or spirit that lives in the body-machine. But a mind is the real you – isn't it?

To observe your brain in action, without you being in control of it, make a notebook about your dreams. Also think about this question: Who is the mysterious "you" who makes and remembers these observations, while the body sleeps?

Making sense of scents

A German poet called Johann Schiller kept over-ripe apples in the drawer of his writing desk. Sniffing the rotten fruit gave Schiller wonderful ideas for his poetry. If this story makes you laugh, imagine these smells:

bread being baked

damp woods in autumn

a freshly-washed towel

grass that has just been cut

rain after days of dry weather in summer

Christmas pudding

your own sweat after a long run

Better still, go around your house and garden, just searching for smells, good ones and bad ones.

Notice how just thinking about smells makes you think of past events in your life. And real smells make you remember vividly – things, people, places, the aroma of your grandmother's scent, a picnic in pine woods.

Yet nobody is sure how the sense of smell works. High inside the spaces inside your nose there are olfactory "smell cells" connected by nerves with an olfactory lobe in your brain.

Smells might be thought of as tiny, different-shaped pieces, so small that they are invisible – called molecules. Depending on the shape of a molecule sniffed or breathed up your nose, the olfactory cells are made to send minute pulses of electricity to your brain. The brain recognizes these signals as, well – whatever they suggest from your memory of past smells – a primrose flower, the scent of a fox, wild garlic, or moth-balls . . .

The journey of a smell

Put a sliced onion, or a splash of scent, on a piece of cloth, in a flat tin with a lid. Let somebody open the tin in a room, as far as possible away from you. Do you notice the smell at once? How long does it take to reach you?

Try this with a classroom filled with children. They all close their eyes and put their hands up when they first notice the smell. They must then keep their hands up. Every 15 seconds, after the tin is opened, count the total number of children with their hands up.

Do these tests support the idea that "smells" are caused by invisible particles which can travel in the air?

Bottled "smellies" — a quiz to find "King (or Queen) Pong"

Buy a dozen small, dark, screw-capped bottles. Half fill each with a different scented liquid. Try orange juice, sour milk, shampoo, limejuice, *very weak* ammonia (**be sure to ask a parent about this**), turpentine, vinegar or beer. Also try solids like tea-leaves, coffee, cocoa, grass-cuttings and cheese.

Plan tests to find out which of your friends has the keenest sense of smell. After each sniff, the top must be replaced on the bottle smelt. Don't forget that identifying scents depends on experience and on remembering names for various odors. Do smokers have a poor sense of smell?

Blindfold the people taking part, to make the tests fairer.

who can smell what?	lavender	rubber bands	orange juice	sour milk	grass-cuttings	lime juice	beer	cheese	peppermint
Johnny	✓	✓		✓	✓		✓	✓	✓
Sharon		✓	✓	✓	✓		✓	✓	
Robert	✓	✓	✓		✓		✓		✓
Samantha		✓		✓	✓	✓			
Mandy	✓	✓	✓	✓	✓	✓	✓	✓	✓
Errol	✓		✓	✓		✓	✓		✓
Katie		✓	✓		✓		✓	✓	✓

Unwrapped scented soap put amongst clothes is said to make them smell sweeter. Keeping a ripe apple in a smoker's car is supposed to lessen the stale smell of cigarette smoke. Do these ideas work? Some scientists think that all smells can be made by varied amounts of only 4 basic smells; these are named "sweet" or fragrant, acid or sour, goaty and burnt. What do you think?

Teasing your taste buds

Use a clean towel to dry your tongue. Poke out your dried tongue. Sprinkle sugar on its tip. You do not taste the sugar. (Guess why, before reading on.)

Afterwards, close your mouth and wet your tongue with saliva – the juices in your mouth. Yes, now you can taste the sugar. There are collections of taste cells in your tongue, called taste buds. Molecules, such as sugar particles, which stimulate taste cells, must be wet for "sensing activity" to occur. The stimulated taste cells transmit electrical signals, via nerves, to your brain – where "the taste of sugar" really happens.

Can you taste the difference between tea sweetened with sugar and tea containing the artificial sweetener saccharine? Can you also taste any difference between margarine and butter? Try the tests when blindfolded.

Confusion between taste and smell

Pinch your nose while you are chewing a few granules of coffee. Although they are moistened with saliva, do they have the full coffee taste? Stop pinching your nose and breathe normally while you go on chewing. Now you should have a richer sense of coffee's flavor.

This little test demonstrates how senses may be linked to provide a flavor. What is called "flavor" in food and drink is the brain interpreting a mixture of sensations. Can you guess why your sense of taste seems to be weaker, when you are suffering from a cold?

People's sense of taste can be confused by comments or suggestions that other people make. If somebody says that meat tastes bad or "off", others will begin to think so too – even if the meat is perfectly good to eat. You can understand this idea better by doing a trick.

Cut a red and a green apple into slices. Put them on separate plates. Say that you can hypnotize people, making them unable to taste any difference between the apples. Blindfold friends, who must also pinch their nostrils. Then listen to what they say when you feed them slices of raw potato (previously hidden away)!

green apple

red apple

Plotting a "taste map" on a tongue

Scientists think that we sense only 4 basic tastes. These are bitter, sweet, salty and acid. Test a person's tongue with solutions which have these tastes. Try to find out if taste buds on different parts of the tongue seem to specialize in bitter, sweet, salty or acid. Use bitter-tasting cold coffee, sugary water, salty water, and watered vinegar. Use separate toothpicks to apply tiny drops of the different tasty solutions to many spots on the front, back and sides of the tongue.

Persons you are testing must rinse out their mouths with water, between each touch of the toothpicks. If you mark the various taste-sensitive spots on a tongue-shaped chart, it should look something like this:

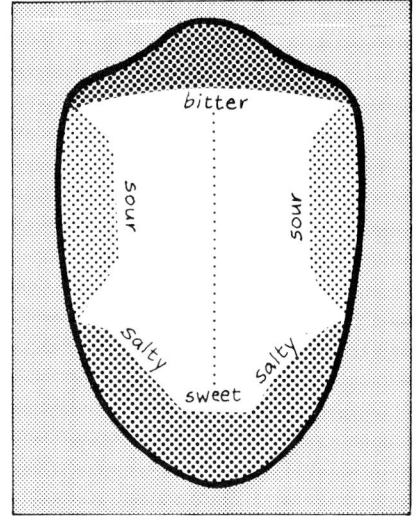

taste map of the tongue

tooth picks   taste map   bitter   sugary   salty   acid

Whilst blindfolded and pinching your nostrils, how many tastes can you identify from amongst, say: cheese, onion, potato, carrot, pear, apple, banana, grape and turnip? A friend can feed you samples on the tips of cocktail sticks. Rinse out your mouth between tastings.

Prepare several glasses of orange squash, each a little stronger than the other. Stir spoonfuls of squash into equal amounts of water. Number the mixtures, in order, weak to strong. Whilst blindfolded, can you put the jumbled glasses back in order, by tasting the squash?

Can you taste an apple, while smelling a slice of pear? (Do this test on a blindfolded friend.)

"Flavor" is obviously a puzzle. It depends on smell, taste – and other senses too. How do hotness or coldness affect flavors? Your mealtime pleasure also depends on sensations of touch and pressure, or "textures" such as crispness and crunchiness. And do you like to *hear* your breakfast cereal going "snap", "crackle" and "pop"?

The ways we touch

Some children like to stroke the black velvet I use to cover my table, when I give a Magic Show. Indeed, few people, given the chance, can resist putting their hands on objects which interest them. Touch is said to be our fifth sense, yet "touch" consists of at least 5 different feelings. They are sensations of heat, cold, pressure, pain, and "light touch" – which you may think of as a sensation of very gentle contact.

In the skin, "free" nerve ends which are not connected with special nerve cells, and arrangements of "organized" nerve endings called bulbs, are sensitive to heat, cold, pain, etc, in ways not at present fully understood by scientists. Nerve endings next to the bottom parts of hairs give you a tickle, or a lively tingling feeling, when somebody lightly strokes your hair, or an insect lands on your cheek. Nerve endings occur closest together on the most sensitive parts of the skin. Shut your eyes while you touch different parts of your skin with the twin points of a hairpin.

The points can be a half inch apart. Test fingertips, palms and backs of your hands, forearm, behind the neck, lips and different parts of your face. **Be careful not to take the hairpin too close to your eyes**. Sometimes you feel two points; at other times the two points feel as if they were only one point. So where do you think the nerve endings of touch are most numerous?

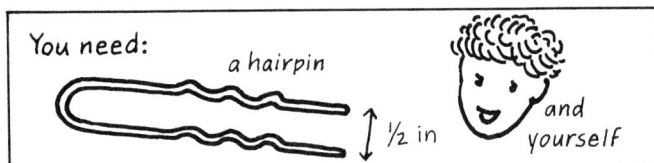

You need: a hairpin ½ in and yourself

When cold feels hot

Sensations of cold can be misinterpreted as heat. When you come in from outdoors in freezing weather, even water from a cold tap feels warm. Sometimes being touched by surprise with a sharp piece of ice can feel like being burnt by the end of a hot stick.

Sensational experiments

Try some more experiments with the hairpin.

1 Open the points and move them across your skin along paths shown by the dotted lines. Explain what you feel as you draw the points down your bare arm and along your fingers. Explain what you feel as you draw the points (aways the same distance apart) across your face.

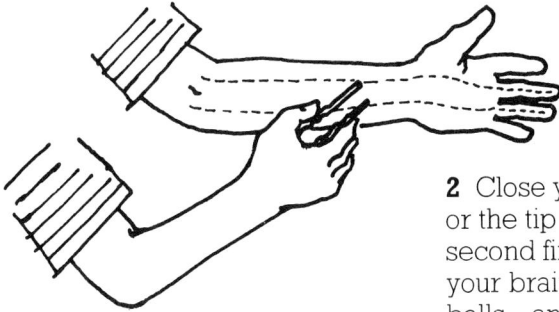

2 Close your eyes while you touch a ping-pong ball or the tip of your nose with your crossed first and second fingertips. When you touch things this way, your brain is confused. You feel that there are two balls – and that you have two noses!

3 Collect materials whose surfaces are interesting to touch: leather, sandpaper, cotton cloth, nylon, silk, blotting-paper, etc. How many of these can you identify with your eyes closed? Tell a horror story in a darkened room, during which you pass around different-feeling objects that *are supposed to be* the nasty things mentioned in the story.

4 Make a set of "worry beads" – about two dozen beads on a loop of string. People have found that handling and "playing" with these helps them to stay calm.

5 Whilst you are blindfolded, what is the smallest piece of paper you can feel when it is dropped a certain distance, to land in the palm of your hand?

Can you identify mystery objects with your bare feet?

Sensations from your ears

Rest your fingertips lightly on a piano or a guitar, when the instrument is being played (or try touching your transistor radio). Feel the gentle tickling sensation. Objects shaking to and fro like this are vibrating. I dare you to discover any sounds being made without something vibrating!

How you hear a sound

Vibrating objects make the air shake to and fro as a series of expanding bubble-shaped waves. These spread out, getting weaker and fainter as they go, until their force is so spent that they fade away. These pressure waves in the air travel into the funnels of your ears, where they hit little fingernail-sized eardrums, making them shake too. Eardrums are like tight skins on drums. An arrangement of tiny bones, connected with the inside of each eardrum, act as levers – increasing the force of the vibrations.

Deep inside your ears are hollow, liquid-filled, snail-shaped organs containing many sensitive hairs. When different sound vibrations make particular hairs vibrate, electrical signals travel along hearing nerves to your brain – where (as by now you can guess) you actually hear. The brain compares the signals with memories of past signals, for which you already have words. Then you can say what you think is causing the sound. Other sounds will be remembered too, but as mysteries – until you learn or invent names for them.

Identify sounds made by different coins when they fall and hit the table. Invent some other tests with many different objects.

Can you hear a whisper made 10 feet away? Invent a test of hearing ability based on the idea of a pin being dropped on a plate. Are both ears equally sensitive to sound?

Your "stereophonic" sense

Shut your eyes or wear a blindfold. Look straight ahead. Listen! Ask a friend to tinkle a little bell from various places around you – but not too close. Point to where you think the sound is coming from each time. It will be hardest to tell, when the bell is directly behind your head, or in front of your chin.

Try this test again, while you are blocking one ear with a hand. (Your friend must keep quiet when moving about.)

How do you think a *pair* of ears detects the direction from which sound waves are coming? Think carefully about this. (Clue: Will the force of waves reaching both ears be the same or different?)

From which position in a room do you get the best impression when you listen to your stereo hi-fi?

Senses which help you to keep your balance

Next to the snail-shaped "inner ears" are the labyrinths, your main sense organs of balance. They consist mainly of 3 curved tubes, fixed at right-angles to each other and partly filled with a liquid. When you move your head, the liquid swirls about in the tubes and washes against hairs joined to nerves, which inform the brain about head movements. Other nerves, from liquid-filled hollow places in the labyrinths, signal the brain with a sense of gravity – telling you "up" from "down". These senses work in the dark, or underwater, but they don't work normally if you happen to be weightless in a spaceship. An overall sensation of balance is also helped by signals coming from cells inside muscles, giving you an impression of your body's posture.

Close your eyes. Quickly turn around 3 times. Open your eyes and try to walk straight. You feel dazed and dizzy. The room seems to be spinning, and you may lurch sideways. Yes, the liquid is still swirling in those tubes!

For how long can you stand on one leg with your eyes closed?

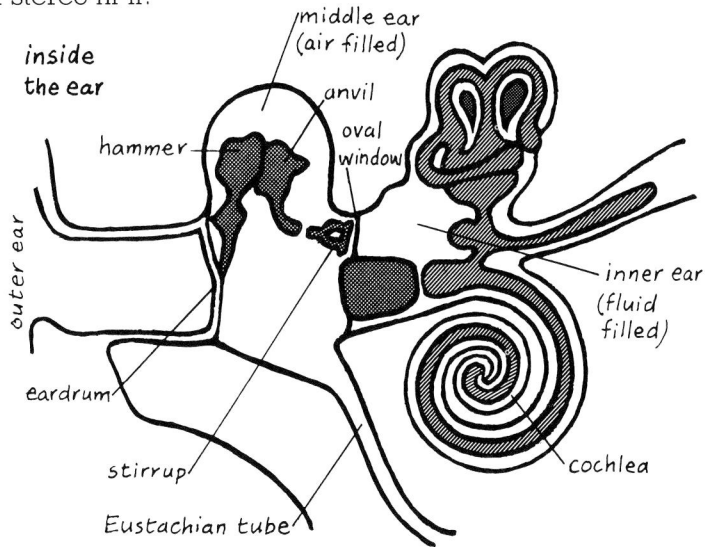

inside the ear

middle ear (air filled)

anvil

oval window

hammer

outer ear

inner ear (fluid filled)

eardrum

cochlea

stirrup

Eustachian tube

A look into your eyes

Look at your eyes in a mirror. Notice the miniature images of yourself in your eyes' black pupils. The pupils are openings, which can get larger or smaller, to let light into your eyes. In the old Latin language, spoken by the Romans, *pupillus* and *pupilla* mean "little boy" and "little girl". Can you guess why an eye's pupil is so-called?

The images you see are reflections in colorless living lenses. These are like transparent windows behind the pupils, letting light go into the dark spaces inside your eyes. Lining the backs of these spaces are the retinas, which consist of cells that react to light coming into your eyes. Nerves connecting the retinal cells with the brain make it possible for you to see.

Do understand that the tiny images of yourself reflected by the pupils are not images focused by your eyes' lenses on their retinas . . . . Strange as it may seem, images on the retinas are focused upside-down! You can make a working model of an eye, to help you understand this idea. Your brain "puts the images the right way up", so that your world looks sensible.

How to make a model of an eye

Paint a large goldfish bowl jet black – *except for* a 3 in-diameter circular window and a 4 x 6 in "eye"-shaped window, directly opposite the round one.

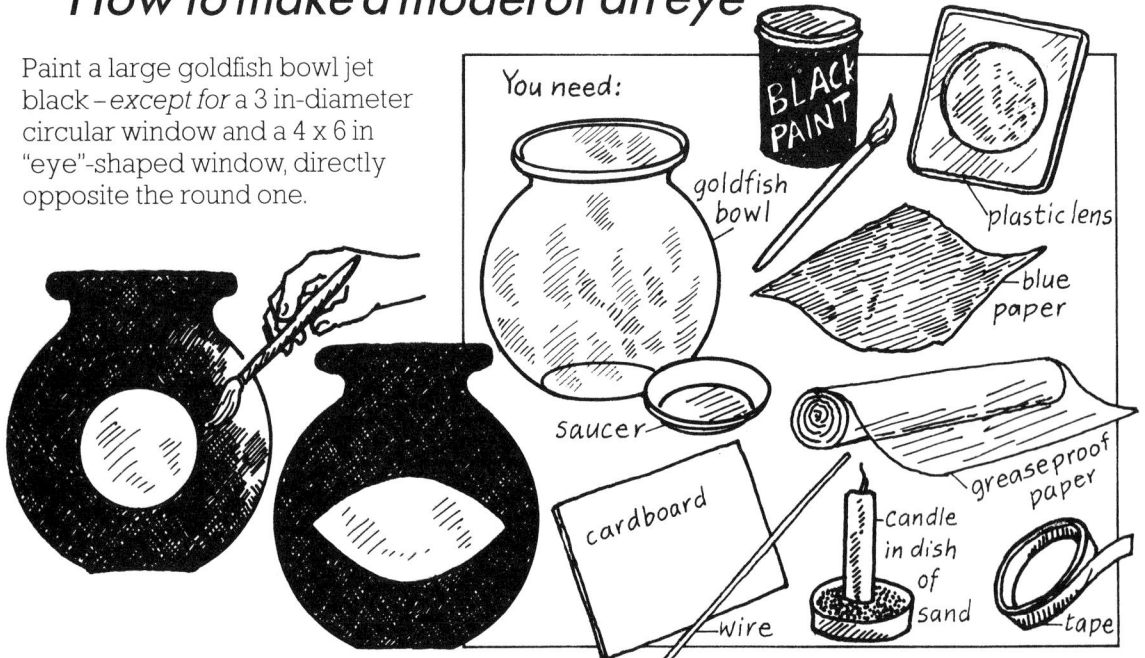

You need:

BLACK PAINT

goldfish bowl

plastic lens

blue paper

saucer

greaseproof paper

cardboard

candle in dish of sand

wire

tape

cut cardboard shape
to fit inside bowl

cut ¾ in -
diameter
hole

stick on
¾ in-wide
ring of
blue paper

Paste a 4 in-diameter greaseproof paper "retina"
screen inside the bowl – behind the circular window.

Cut a cardboard shape to fit loosely upright inside the
middle of the glass "eyeball". This will divide the
hollow bowl into two spaces.

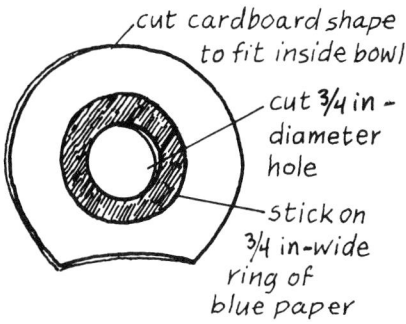

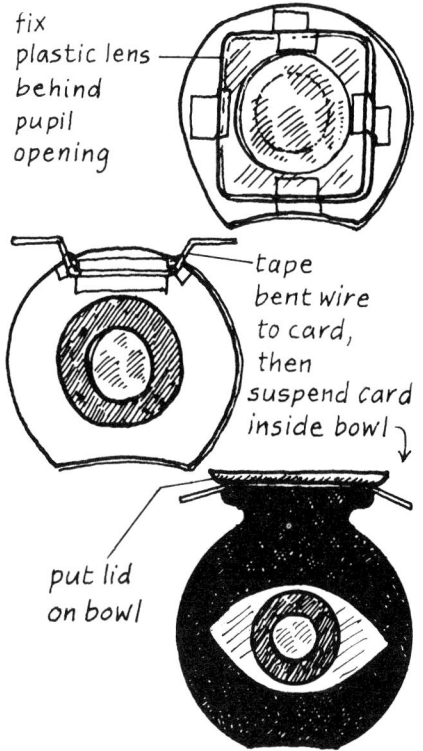

Make a ¾ in-diameter hole in the center of this card,
to represent the eye's pupil. Then stick a ¾ in-wide
ring of blue paper around the hole, to form an "iris".

Fix a plastic lens behind the pupil opening, using
sticky tape – you need a fat-in-the-middle double
convex lens. Plastic "magnifiers" can sometimes be
bought very cheaply at a toyshop, stationer's or
Woolworths. A suitable lens will have a focal length
of between 2 and 4 in.

Use sticky tape to fix a bent wire to the cardboard, so
that the wire can be used to suspend the lens-iris-
pupil combination inside the bowl.

Dangle the lens-iris-pupil across the middle of the
bowl – with the iris facing the eye-shaped window.
Rest a black-painted lid (an old saucer will do) on top
of the bowl.

fix
plastic lens
behind
pupil
opening

tape
bent wire
to card,
then
suspend card
inside bowl

put lid
on bowl

Test the model in a dimly-lit room. Put a lighted candle in a shallow dish of
sand (for safety's sake) in front of the eye's front part – the transparent "cornea"
in real life. Then, while you are looking at the back of the artificial retina
screen *from behind the model*, move the wire suspender to and fro. Suddenly
you see a bright miniature upside-down image of the candle.

In a real eye its lens can be made fatter or thinner by
muscles, to help the lens to get images in sharp focus.

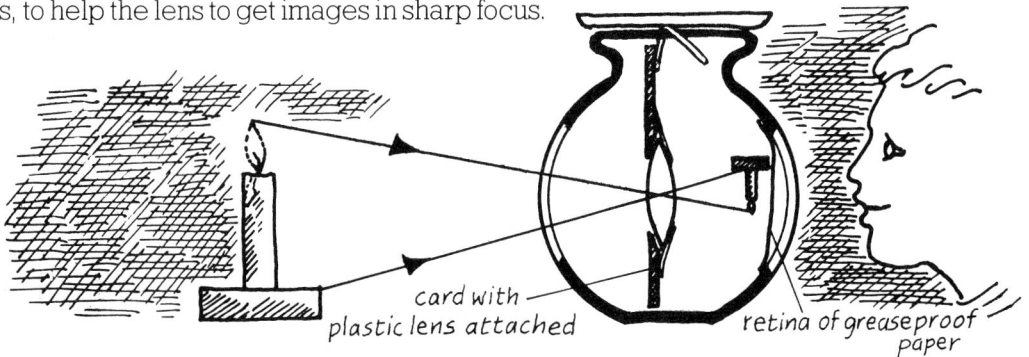

card with
plastic lens attached

retina of greaseproof
paper

17

Eye tests

Protection for your eyes

Your eyes are sphere-shaped, about the size of ping-pong balls. If you get a chance to look at a skull, notice the deep eye-sockets, where the eyes were protected by hard bone. Feel your own eye-sockets, and feel the forward projecting bony brows and the upper cheek bones. Your eyes are also protected by eyelids – if you close your eyes and stare at a bright light, you see the redness of their blood supply.

Eyelids act like shutters, and as "windscreen wipers". Wetted by tears from glands under the outer eyebrows, your eyelids can act to wash away harmful specks of dirt. Tears also contain a substance which kills germs.

The tears drain through little holes in the inner corners of your eyes, to trickle down inside your nose. When your eyes are in danger, the eyelids close automatically, without you having to think about it – an action which is called a reflex. Ask a friend to stand some distance away, with a transparent plastic folder held to cover his or her eyes. Watch those eyes when you throw paper balls at them!

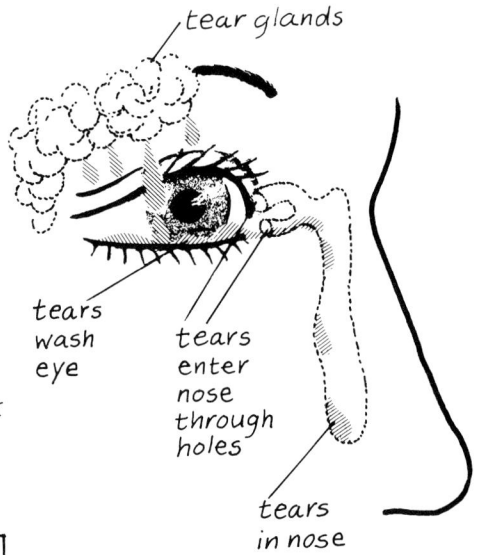

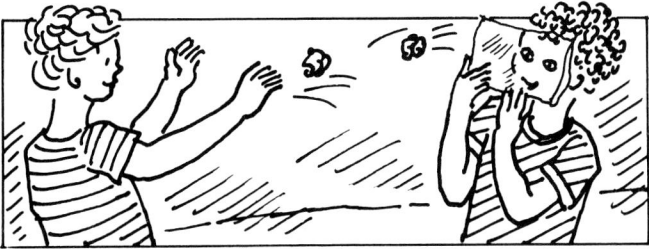

tear glands

tears wash eye

tears enter nose through holes

tears in nose

Which is the eye you prefer to use?

Most people use one eye more than the other. The eye preferred is called the dominant eye. To tell which is your dominant eye, hold your thumb out at arm's length and stare past it, at an object – such as a toy bear – on the far side of a room. Close your left eye. If your right eye still sees the thumb and bear in line, you are right-eyed. (If now you open your left eye and close your right eye, the thumb appears to shift to the right.) These results would be reversed for a left-eyed person.

A curious discovery

The iris of your eye is really a ring of muscle. In bright light this muscle makes the pupil opening smaller. Too bright a light is dazzling, as you know from experience. A smaller pupil lets in less light. In dim light the iris makes the pupil larger. When lighting is poor, your eye must let in more light in order to see properly. These changes in the size of the pupil are reflex actions.

When the daylight is fading, look in a mirror to observe the sizes of your pupils. Turn on a light, stare at the light for about twenty seconds – then inspect your pupils again. The dark openings will be smaller now.

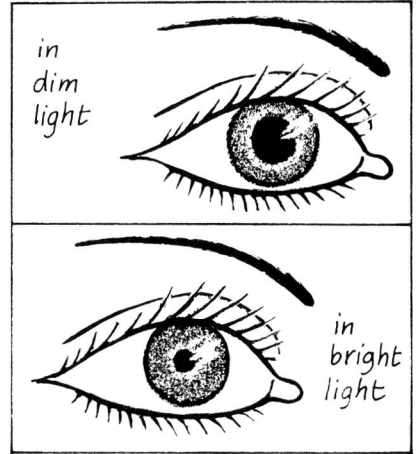

in dim light

in bright light

Merchants found that the pupils of persons who badly wanted to buy their goods, became larger. The merchants used this knowledge to get good profits for themselves. You might wish to investigate this curious information.

You could put a very interesting picture amongst several very boring ones. Mix them up, so that you don't know the order they are in. Stand facing a person and look into their eyes, while you show them the pictures, one at a time. You must still not see the pictures yourself. When the interesting picture appears, you can expect the person's pupils to get larger. Scientists found that a cheerful baby amongst boring landscapes was a good picture to use with women. Men showed most interest in a picture of a nude! Can you guess an explanation for this reflex action?

Why do we need two eyes? Surely we see perfectly well with one? Close an eye, while you try to thread a needle. Close an eye, and hold your arms out straight, while you try to put the top back on your pen. Two eyes help us to see in 3D – they give us "in depth" stereo-vision.

19

CIRCUS OF SENSATION

Contrary "pin-up"

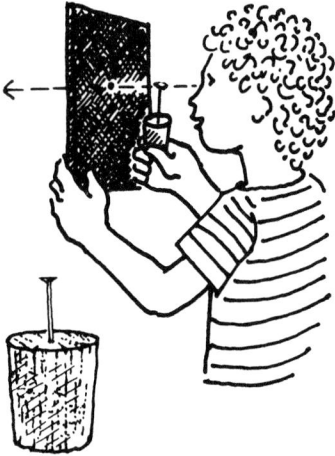

Make a pinhole in a piece of black paper. Stick the pin in a small cork. Look through the hole at a bright light – but **never** the sun! Use the cork as a holder, when you put the head of the pin close to the eye you are using. It's "magic"! The pin seems to be upside-down.

Light casts a *shadow* of the pin through the lens of your eye – on to the retina. The pin is too close and poorly lit for it to be focused by the lens to form an *image*. Your brain is so used to making upside-down *images* seem upright, that it acts in a routine way – making you see the upright shadow as if it were inverted.

Ambiguities

Where is the slice that is missing from this cake? It appears when you look at the plate upside down. When you inspect the picture one way or the other, your brain makes the most sensible judgement of what the drawing means. Look at the other picture.

Do you see an old woman, or a pretty young girl? This picture is cleverly drawn to be ambiguous (it can be interpreted in more than one way).

You may find other examples of drawings like these. I challenge you to *invent* an ambiguous picture.

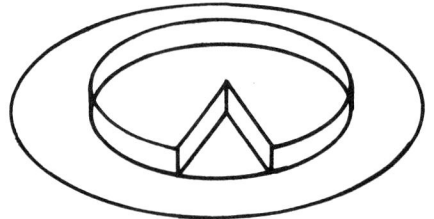

Reading by touch

With your eyes closed, can you identify numbers, letters and words, "drawn" by your friend using a finger, on the palm of your hand? Test other parts of your body. Try the soles of your feet. Can you exchange messages this way? Try to identify a square, a triangle and a circle – formed by bending cardboard strips – when their edges are pressed against your skin.

Perhaps you know a blind person who will read to you from a book printed in Braille letters.

You are an unreliable thermometer

You need 3 bowls, one filled with water as hot as you can bear, one containing water with a few ice cubes floating in it, and one filled with lukewarm water. Put the warm water between the other two bowls. Dry your hands. Then soak one hand in the hot and the other hand in the icy water. When both hands tingle, dip them both in the tepid water. What do you feel? Amazing, isn't it?

hot water

lukewarm water

ice cold water

Human feelings of temperature are unreliable – they depend upon whether we felt "hot" or "cold" before making a judgement.

A prank with a plank

Stand a blindfolded person on a plank. Tell him that he must walk along the plank, but that you will raise the plank first. Four friends who know this trick will be ready as assistants. Your plank walker must not know what you are going to do.

Children at each end of the plank lift it about a foot above the floor (no more!) Meanwhile, two other children support the blindfolded person's hands. As the plank is slowly raised, the hand supporters must bend their knees. The plank walker will have a weird sensation of being very high up – and will move along the plank with extreme care!

When your body acts like a robot

Try this test on friends who are used to your tricks. Ask them to close their eyes and hold out their bare arm. Then touch them suddenly on the underside of the arm, using an ice cube, previously kept hidden.

Notice how quickly the arm is jerked away. There may be cries of pain! Explain that you are investigating a reflex action – and thank your friends for being unsuspecting guinea-pigs in your research.

A reflex is another kind of automatic action. The body acts like a robot – before you have time to think. This is usually a good thing, especially when the reflex is caused by something that can kill (the sudden appearance of an approaching truck, for example).

The nasty surprise with the ice made nerves in your friends' skins send urgent cold and pain signals to their spinal cords. Nerves from their spines immediately signalled to muscles, making their arms pull away.

Reflexes happen to you all the time. "Happen to you" is correct, because you do not act on purpose.

Steam, bikes and knee-jerks

You jerk away a hand when it is touched by steam coming from a boiling kettle. If you waste half a second "making up your mind" to act, the burn from the scalding steam is much worse. Yet, while the reflex is happening, other nerves carry pulses to your brain – where you suffer the pain. Then you may or may not think you are in control, when you yell "Ouch!"

Many reflexes have to be learned. If you ride a bike, remember how it was in the beginning. You kept falling off! Now your body can manage the bicycle – like a robot – while you have a deep conversation.

Try a reflex action you had no need to learn – a doctor may do this test on you. Begin by sitting comfortably, with your knees crossed. Then hit yourself a sharp blow, using the edge of a hand – aiming just below the top knee-cap. If you hit the right spot, the knee jerks up. You won't be able to help it.

Here are two good tricks, both connected with reflexes. The first illustrates how people tend to "jump to conclusions", without thinking. The second trick illustrates "force of habit". Try them on your friends.

Sum mistake

Cover the sum with a black card. Move the card down, to expose the numbers, one by one. Keep adding them together. Get on with it, without pausing to think. I have made the addition very easy.

Call out the answer. Did you shout "Five thousand"? Most people do. *Now check the figures more thoughtfully.*

$$1000$$
$$40$$
$$1000$$
$$10$$
$$1000$$
$$40$$
$$1000$$
$$10$$

Topsy-turvy

Hold up a $1 bill, with Washington's portrait showing upright.

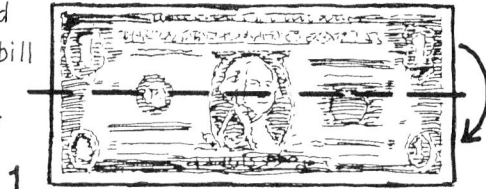

fold
$1 bill
in
half

1

Fold the money in half by bringing its top edge forward and down, to meet the bottom edge (Stage **1**).

Fold the bundle in half again, by bending the right edge *backwards* to meet the left edge (Stage **2**).

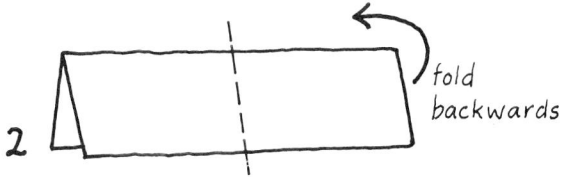

2

fold
backwards

Finally fold the bundle in half again, by bending the right edge *across the front*, to meet the left edge (Stage **3**).

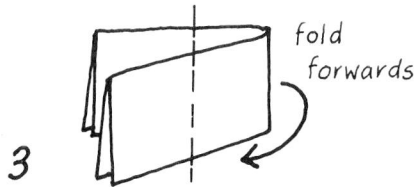

3

fold
forwards

Quickly unfold the note. Washington's portrait should appear upside-down, especially if you are right-handed.

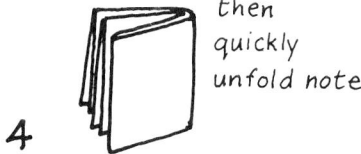

4

then
quickly
unfold note

You made the "magic" possible at Stage **2**, when you would naturally have folded the paper across the front – as you did at Stage **3**.

Does this work for everybody? Investigate.

Copy this funny face on a piece of paper, and fold it in the same way as the $1 bill. See what happens.

Are you "quick on the draw"?

Imagine relaxing while riding your bicycle down a steep hill in the country on a windy day. Suddenly a huge tree falls right in front of you.

You need:
1 Time to see what's happened.
2 Time to decide what to do.
3 Time to avoid hitting the tree.

These times add up to your reaction time – the total time it takes to sense a danger and prevent it from harming you. Jet-fighter pilots, racing-car drivers and soldiers in battle, all depend on rapid reaction times to stay alive.

Test your reaction time. Get a friend to time how long it takes you to touch every numbered square in the correct order. 9 seconds is about average (the time most people take), 7 is very good, but 5 seconds makes you a jet-fighter pilot!

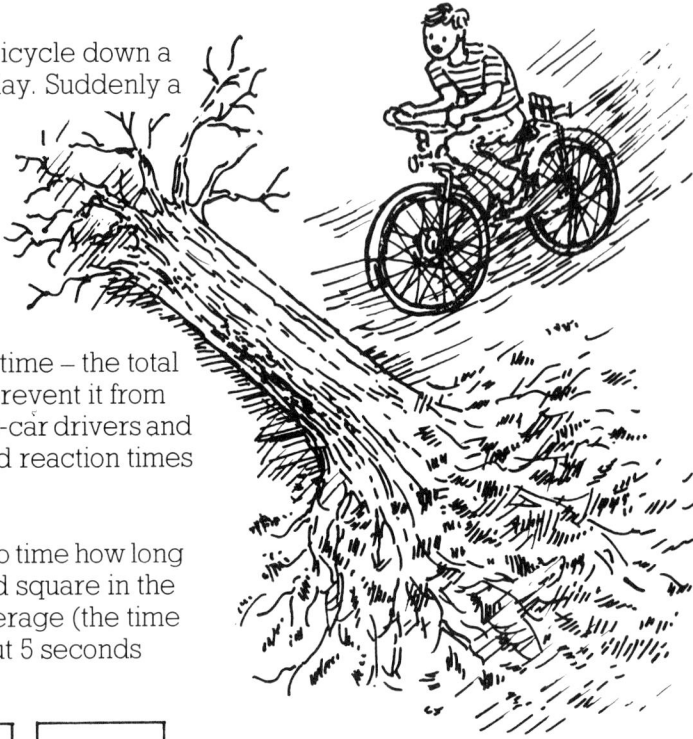

4	3	10	12
6	11	8	9
1	7	2	5

Games

1 Rest a nickel on the back of a hand. Twist the wrist, to tip off the coin – and try to catch the coin *with the same hand*. It's not easy. How many times do you succeed in 5 tries? Practice. Does your score improve? Try the game with your other hand.

2 In a game with a partner, hold out the palm of your hand. The other person drops a penny from a certain height, over your hand. You have to move away your hand before the coin hits it. Vary the game, making the falling distance less.

A "fiver" test

Ask a person to open a finger
and thumb, 1.5 in apart, to
resemble a crab's pincers.
Dangle a $5 bill or a similar
shape of paper between them.
Can your friend grab the paper,
when, without warning, you drop
it? People nearly always fail –
their reaction times are too slow.

Distance of fall (in)	Time of fall (seconds)
1.0	.078
1.5	.090
2.0	.101
2.5	.115
3.0	.128
3.5	.136
4.0	.143
4.5	.153
5.0	.163
5.5	.169
6.0	.175
6.5	.184
7.0	.192
7.5	.197
8.0	.202
8.5	.212
9.0	.217
9.5	.221
10.0	.226

Use the basic idea to get an actual time. Replace the
"fiver" with a 18 inch ruler. Dangle the beginning of
the ruler between another person's opened finger
and thumb. When you let go, it is possible for most
people to catch and hold the ruler. See how many
inches the ruler has fallen before being caught – and
read the time in seconds from the chart.

How quickly can a person get a foot out of the way,
without it being hit by a ball you drop from directly
over it? The least distance the ball has to fall will give
the reaction time – if you look on the chart.

Reaction time for a group of people

Stand with a group of friends in a circle. Face outwards and join hands. Person
number one starts a stop-watch or other timer. At the same instant, that
person squeezes the hand of the second person. Each person in the circle
"passes on" the squeeze from hand to hand.

Meanwhile, number one has put the timer in the other hand and grasped the
hand of the last member of the circle. When number one feels a squeeze from
the last person, the timer is stopped. Does the group's reaction time get
better after several tests? Are girls better at this than boys? Invent different
variations.

Learning to love your skeleton

Imagine the skeleton inside your body – "Dem bones!" Squeeze yourself all over. Use the picture to help you identify, by touch, all the bones I have labelled. Without a bony framework, you would find it impossible to walk, run, jump about, or use your hands. Your body would flop down like a heap of jelly.

Unlike the rigid framework of a modern city building, the skeleton is articulated – it has moveable joints. Wrist bones slide against each other at "glide joints". Other joints act like door hinges, "balls" in sockets, and pivots (pins around which things turn, such as the pivot joint of a wheel and axle). Can you find them?

The lower jaw bone is the only moveable bone in your skull. Other tough bones of the skull form a hard "box" to hold and protect your brain. Important parts of your ears are embedded in the skull. Try an impressive demonstration to show how a dome – the shape of your skull – is incredibly strong.

skull
collar bone (clavicle)
lower jaw
neck vertebra
shoulder blade (scapula)
sternum
humerus
ribs
lumbar vertebra
pelvis
radius
ulna
carpals
femur
knee-cap (patella)
tibia
fibula
tarsals

You need an egg and a plastic bag. Each end of the egg is dome-shaped (although the egg is a great deal more delicate than the skull).

Clasp your hands together by interlocking your fingers – with the ends of the egg pressing into the palms of your hands. Hold your hands inside the bag, just in case the egg should break. Then squeeze, to try to crush the egg, with all your might. Even an adult will not smash the egg by squeezing its domes, end to end!

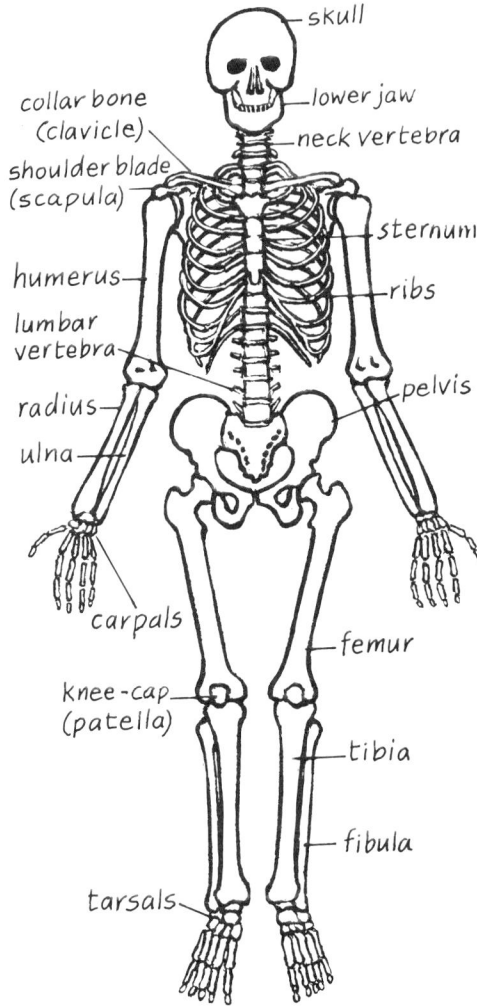

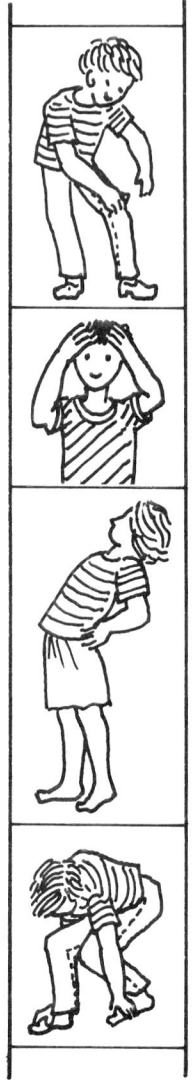

squee-e-e-eze

egg

plastic bag

Straighten your arm. Gently squeeze the front of your upper arm, while bending the elbow. Feel the biceps muscle getting fatter, as its bundles of long cells shorten to pull up the arm. When you straighten the arm, you should be able to feel the triceps muscle behind your arm getting fatter. As the biceps shortens, the cell bundles in your triceps relax. Most of your muscles that move bones act in pairs, and you have direct control over them – you can make them do what you want them to. Other muscles, such as those lining the intestines and heart, work automatically.

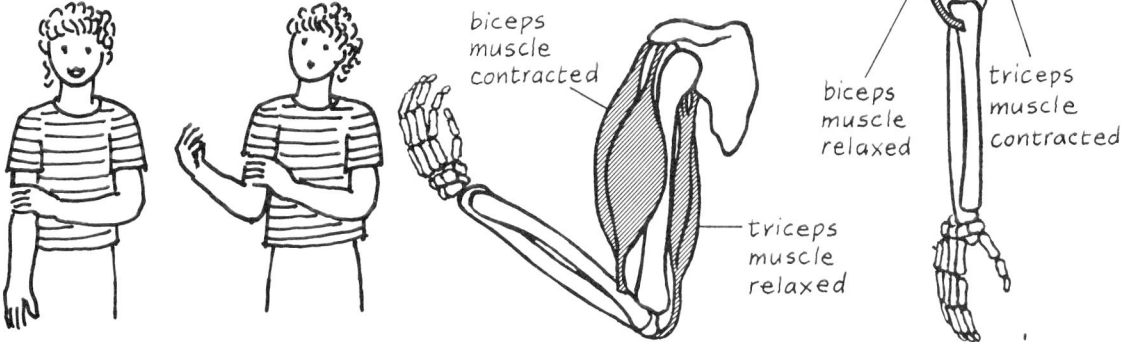

biceps muscle contracted

biceps muscle relaxed

triceps muscle contracted

triceps muscle relaxed

Muscles and posture

The ways you stand, "hold yourself" and sit are called body posture. Your posture depends on how you let muscles act on your skeleton. Good posture makes you feel fit. Bad posture is ugly – you are not making the most of your attractiveness; it also causes aches and pains, because bad posture means that your body is hunched up and squashed.

Check that, when standing, you have ankles, hips, shoulders and ears in line. Ears, shoulders and hips should also be in line when you are sitting. The weight of your thighs should be supported by the chair, and the weight of your feet by the ground. Avoid sitting or standing with your legs crossed.

the right way to sit and stand

WRONG

RIGHT

When you bend to pick up a heavy load, never keep your legs straight – you could hurt your back. Keep your back straight while you bend your knees, then stoop. As you take the load, lean backwards a little. Then lift, by straightening the knees.

How many times can you squeeze a clothes peg, in half a minute? Without resting, try the test two or three times again. Do you find that your muscles get tired? Can you improve your skill at this game, with practice?

Skin games

Nearly all the "house-dust" in your home is probably made from billions of worn-out cells, shed from the surfaces of people's germ-proof, waterproof, touch-, cold- and heat-sensitive body wrappings – their skins.

How much skin do you have?

Get a very rough idea by letting a friend draw around your body's outline – you must be lying down on a strip made by pasting newspapers together. If you cut out two such shapes and hang them side by side, they will give an *impression* of the total skin area.

Can you work out this area in square inches? This should be easy if you can afford to buy enough inch square graph paper.

A more accurate way to find the area of your skin is to measure the surface piece by piece – by, for example, rolling paper around arms, legs, fingers, etc – and then add up all the measurements.

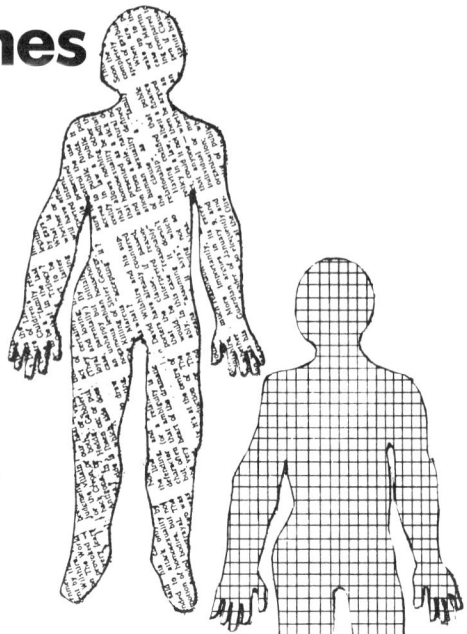

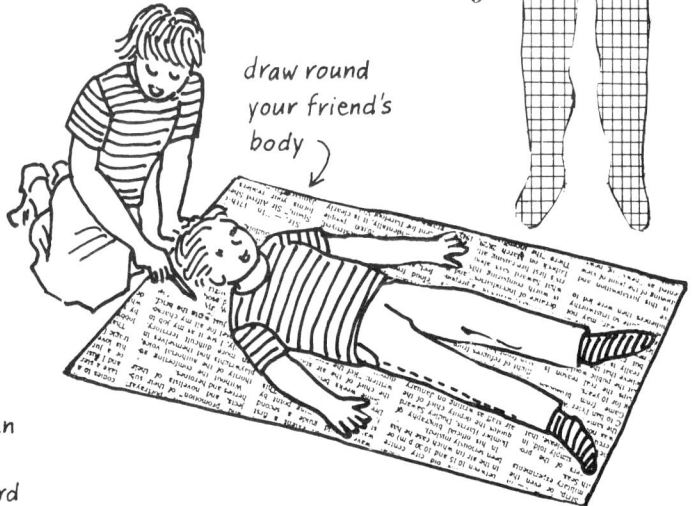

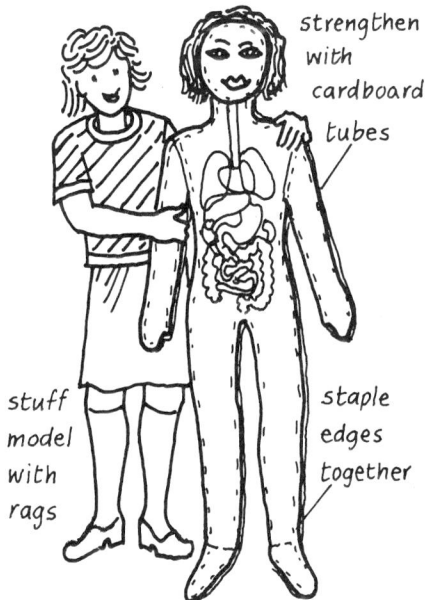

draw round your friend's body

strengthen with cardboard tubes

stuff model with rags

staple edges together

How to be a paper doll

If you are prepared to be patient, you can construct a life-size, brown-paper "doll" of yourself. Make two outlines, but much fatter than the true outlines you made before. The neck and where arms and legs join with the body should be especially wide – these places can be strengthened with cardboard tubes. Staple the outlines together while stuffing the model with rags.

Draw your face on the doll. Then you could draw some of your body parts on the paper skin – heart, lungs, stomach, etc–showing their sizes and positions. Find the information you need in biology books.

Fingerprinting

The Chinese used fingerprints to sign legal papers many centuries before they were used in Europe to identify criminals. A police expert recognizes four basic fingerprint patterns: arches, loops, whorls and composites (mixtures of the other three types) – yet no two persons' prints are ever exactly alike, even those of identical twins.

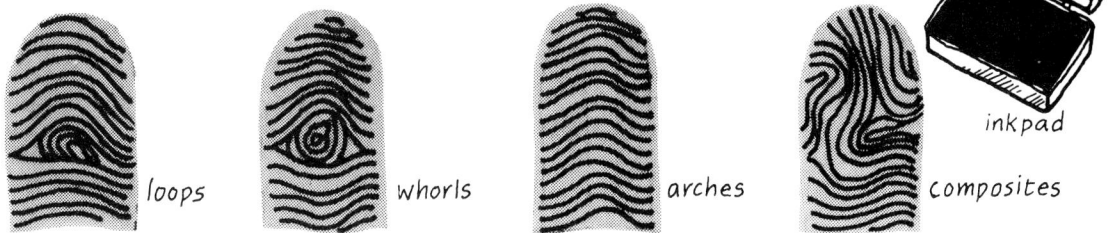

loops   whorls   arches   composites   inkpad

Use an ink-pad (which you can buy at a stationer's) to make prints from your own fingers. Prints are taken, for record purposes, by *rolling* the inky fingers on to special cards. Which of the basic patterns do your fingerprints have? Compare prints made by the "same" fingers from either hand. Can you discover examples of all the basic patterns amongst your friends' prints?

Take a thumb print from each child in your class at school. Label each with its owner's name. Ask your teacher to appoint one child to be a burglar. She must do this secretly and record the person's print on a white card. How quickly can the other children identify the criminal? The first child detective to succeed qualifies as Sherlock Holmes.

A magical mystery

Doctors sometimes use methods that seem like magic to make warts "go away". Here is such a method. If you have warts on your skin, wait until full moon, then touch each wart with a separate small piece of raw meat – and bury the meat in your garden. As the meat rots in the ground, your warts should wither and drop off. **Parents may wish to supervise this harmless experiment**. We don't know how it works, but somebody will find a scientific explanation one day. Perhaps you will.

How you digest your food

Munch and swallow 3 dry *sugar-free* cracker biscuits in just one minute. I challenge you! It's a safe bet that you and your friends will fail, because you are not able to make enough saliva, or "spit", to make the biscuit slippery enough to swallow.

Saliva also contains an enzyme, a substance which breaks big molecules into smaller molecules. The enzyme in saliva breaks big starch molecules into smaller sugar ones – they need to be small to get into your blood. If you start with an empty mouth and keep on chewing a piece of cracker, it begins to taste sweet. Can you guess why?

The tunnel through your body

Beginning with your mouth and ending with the anus, where unused food comes out when you go to the lavatory, a winding tube-like "tunnel" – 10 yards long in an adult – goes right through your body. Just think, most of the food you swallow never actually enters your body in the form in which you ate it! Nearly all of it must be digested first. Different enzymes act on different substances in your food, as it passes through your stomach and into the beginning of your intestines.

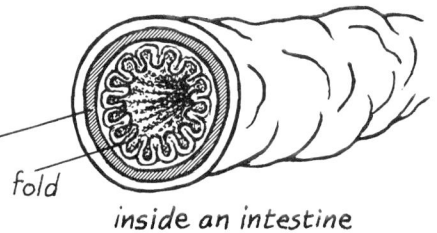

push marble along tube

muscle - helps move food along

fold

inside an intestine

You have enough acid in your stomach to dissolve a nail – it helps to break up fats, and kills most of the germs you swallow. Stomach muscles squash and churn the food. Muscles in the intestines squeeze the digesting food along. See how this happens by squeezing a big marble along inside a rubber tube. About 3 or 4 hours after a heavy meal, lie in a warm bath, with your tummy just above the water. Watch for slight heaving actions of your intestines.

BATH MAT

Mainly in the first part of the intestines, small molecules get through the wall of the tunnel, into your bloodstream. The lining of the intestines has a huge area – as much as 9 square yards! This is possible because the lining has many folds. To understand how a huge surface can be packed into a small space, fold a piece of paper into accordion pleats.

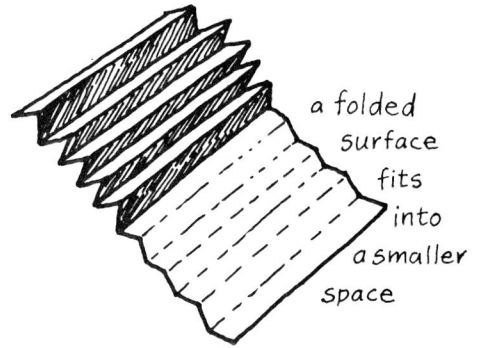

a folded surface fits into a smaller space

Facts you may often have wondered about

Some molecules get into your bloodstream without being changed. If these happen to be of no use, they are got rid of with other body wastes when you urinate or "pass water". While getting rid of your urine, you may have noticed a faint smell, reminding you of a meal you ate.

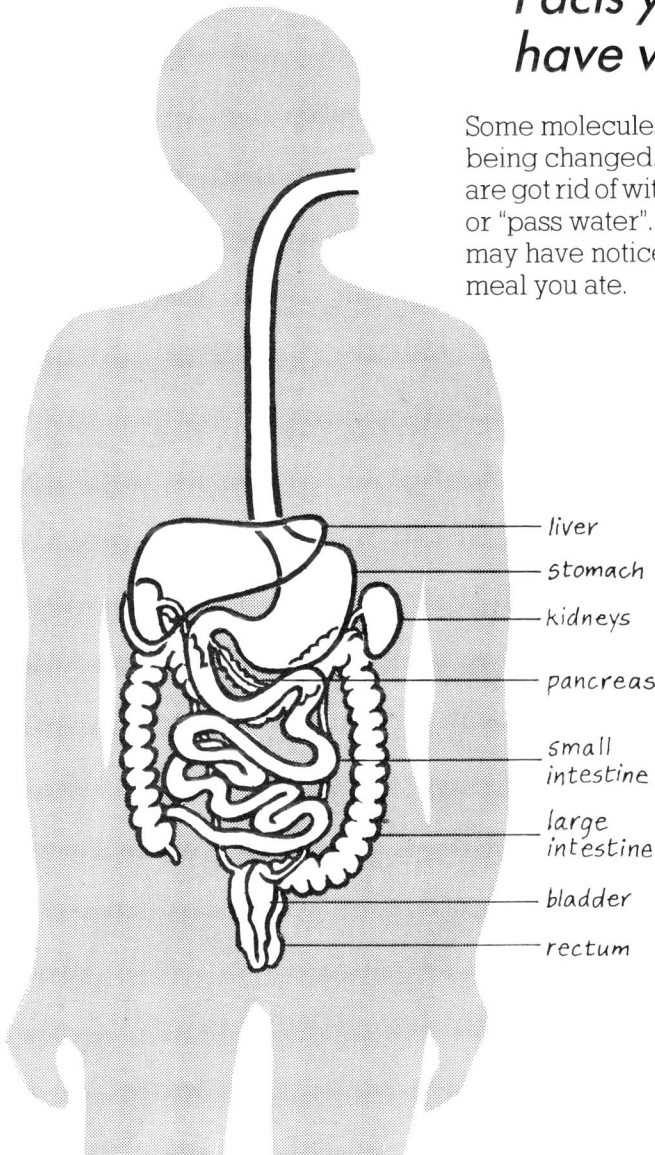

liver
stomach
kidneys
pancreas
small intestine
large intestine
bladder
rectum

Unused food coming from the anus smells unpleasant, especially if you have eaten foods such as cabbage, cauliflower, onions and beans. Billions of germ-like, but harmless bacteria live in the end part of your intestines. When they feed on unused food, they produce nasty-smelling gas. This gas, with air you swallow with meals, might cause you embarrassment when, as everyone has to do, you "break wind".

Did you know that you eat enough food to feed an "army"? These are the bacteria living inside you – they add up to a bigger number than all the people in the world!

Why you breathe

Without fresh air you would die within minutes. Air breathed in goes to your lungs – in your chest – where oxygen from the air can get into your bloodstream. Waste substances from the blood, mainly carbon dioxide and water, pass from the blood into the air you breathe out. Breathe on a cold window, to see the water from your breath condense as mist.

Blood carries oxygen all over your body, to living cells, where the oxygen is essential for a slow kind of burning, to set free the energy from sugar. Of course, the sugar came from food you ate. The cells use sugar as "fuel" to make them work and grow.

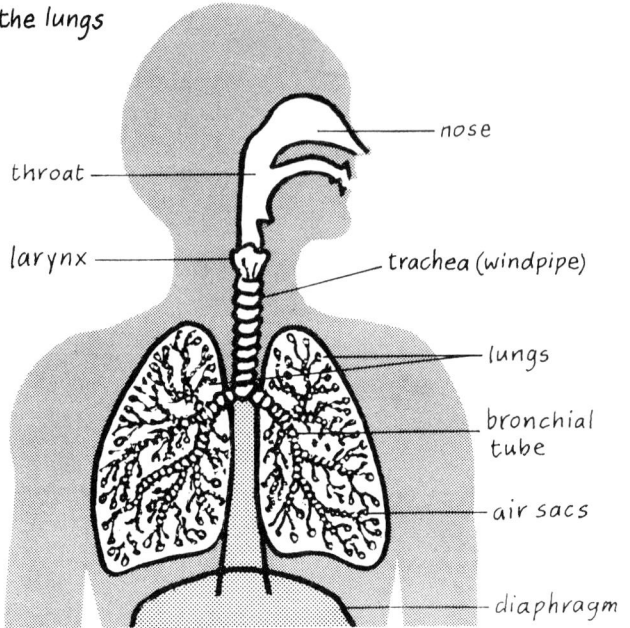

the lungs

nose

throat

larynx

trachea (windpipe)

lungs

bronchial tube

air sacs

diaphragm

This produces wastes, which are carried back in the blood to your lungs, for breathing out.

Lungs are like wrapped-up sponges, containing millions of little spaces in which stale air is exchanged for fresh air. When you breathe in, the space in your chest gets bigger and the lungs can take up more room – so air pushes in through your nose and mouth. To make the chest space bigger, a thick muscle under your chest pushes down on your stomach and intestines, at the same time as other muscles spread your ribs.

When you breathe out, the thick muscle moves up again, while your ribs press inwards – so air is squashed out of your lungs.

How to make a model lung

This model gives a rough idea of how the "thick muscle", called the diaphragm, helps to make the lungs larger and smaller when you breathe. You need the top 5 in of a plastic lemonade bottle. Poke in a balloon to represent a lung. (Catch the balloon neck on the mouth of the bottle.) Tape a big piece cut from another balloon, to cover the large opening and to represent the diaphragm.

You need:

tape

plastic lemonade bottle

balloons

cut
the top
5 in from
the plastic
bottle

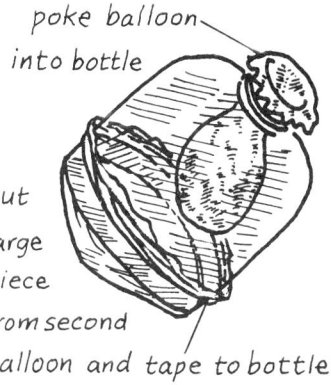

poke balloon
into bottle

cut
large
piece
from second
balloon and tape to bottle

Grip a fold from the "diaphragm". Watch what happens to the "lung" when you pull down and push up this rubber sheet. Can you figure out how the model works? Of course, real lungs fill the space.

pull down the
"diaphragm"

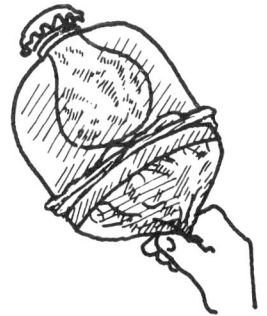

How much air can your lungs hold?

Sink the biggest possible sweet or pickles jar in a sink or big bowl of water. Stand the jar upside-down – it should be filled with water, but no water will run out yet. Poke one end of a yard-long plastic tube – such as wine-makers use – inside the bottom of the jar.

Take a deep breath and blow into the tube. Air from your lungs forces down the water-level, to make a trapped bubble. Mark the water-level with a rubber band. If you take the deepest breath you can, and blow all this air into the jar, the size of the bubble represents how much air your lungs can hold.

Use this equipment, with different-colored rubber bands, to compare how much air your friends' lungs can hold. How could you measure these amounts?

Sensing mysteries of the heart

If you hold one end of a short cardboard tube to about the middle of a friend's chest, and you listen at the other end, you should hear the lub-dup, lub-dup sound of a heart pump at work – between 70 and 80 beats a minute, but it can be more if you are very young. Assume that it beats 72 times a minute and that a person might live for 70 years. How many beats (very roughly!) might there be in a lifetime? Work it out with pencil, paper and your calculator.

Your body's main transport system

About the size of your fist, your muscular heart forces blood around your body – away from itself through arteries, along thin tubes called capillaries amongst the tiny cells, and back to itself through veins. First the blood goes to your lungs, to collect oxygen and get rid of waste gases. Then it goes all over your body, including the wall of your intestines – through which food molecules and water get into the bloodstream.

As the blood goes through your kidneys, in your lower back, waste substances dissolved in it are filtered out, to be got rid of in the urine when you go to the lavatory. Blood also carries sweat, a watery substance, to little sweat-glands in your skin. Some waste is disposed of in sweat, but sweating also helps to keep you from getting too hot.

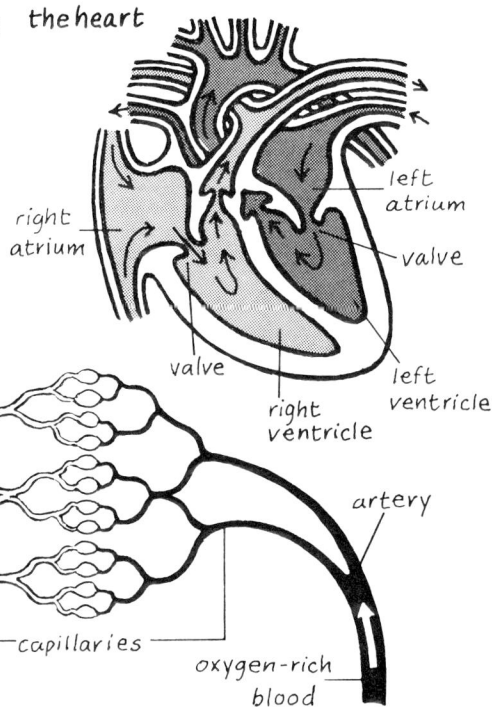

the heart

right atrium

left atrium

valve

valve

right ventricle

left ventricle

vein

artery

capillaries

oxygen-poor blood

oxygen-rich blood

How to take a pulse

The usual way a nurse measures your heart beat is to take a pulse. Hold out one hand. Feel gently with fingertips of the opposite hand. Touch your wrist near the beginning of the thumb. Don't hurry. You should be able to feel a slight throbbing (blood passing through an artery – throbbing being produced by the heart pumping). Count how many beats there are in one minute. That will be your "pulse".

What happens to your pulse when you exercise?

Take your pulse while sitting quietly, resting.
Take it again after running very fast.
Wait 5 minutes, resting – then take your pulse again.

Can you explain the results of these tests?
Compare your results with tests on your friends.

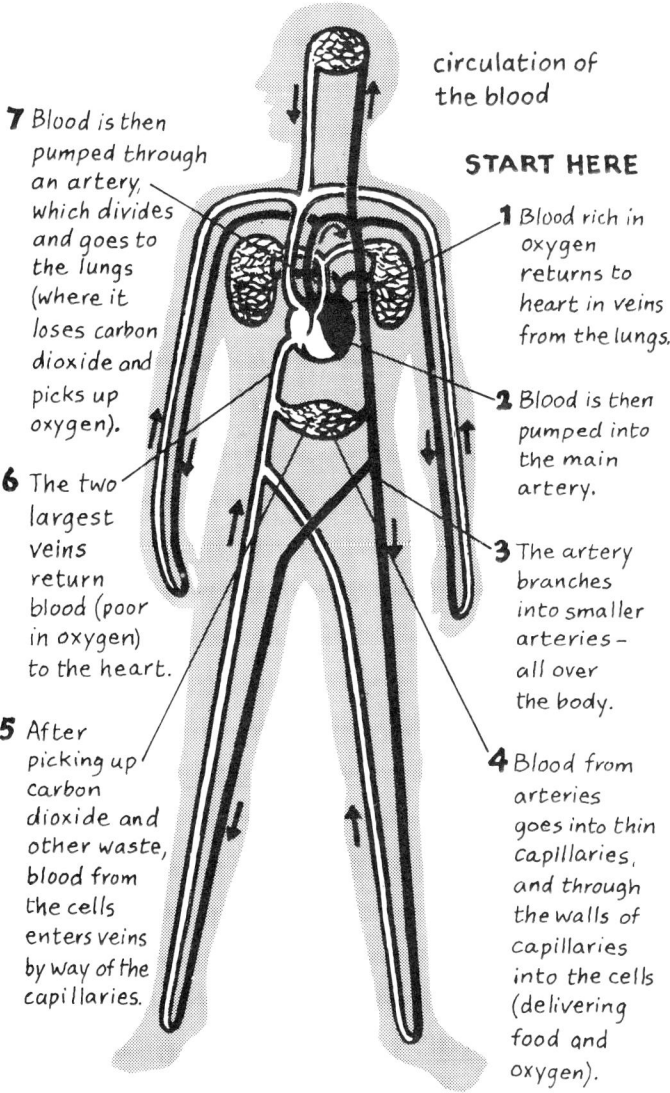

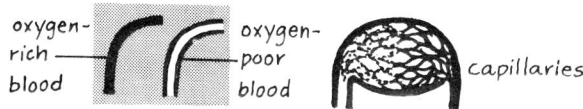

circulation of the blood

START HERE

1 Blood rich in oxygen returns to heart in veins from the lungs.

2 Blood is then pumped into the main artery.

3 The artery branches into smaller arteries – all over the body.

4 Blood from arteries goes into thin capillaries, and through the walls of capillaries into the cells (delivering food and oxygen).

5 After picking up carbon dioxide and other waste, blood from the cells enters veins by way of the capillaries.

6 The two largest veins return blood (poor in oxygen) to the heart.

7 Blood is then pumped through an artery, which divides and goes to the lungs (where it loses carbon dioxide and picks up oxygen).

oxygen-rich blood — oxygen-poor blood

capillaries

Healthy eating

Feel which of your teeth chop or tear or crush your food, to increase the surfaces for enzymes to act on.

Bacteria living in your mouth change food fragments into acid, which rots your teeth. Crispy raw carrot and apple help to scrub away these pieces of food. Look at your teeth in a mirror, after eating black licorice – then again, after munching an apple.

Acid from fizzy drinks can also damage your teeth. Next time you lose a tooth, put it in fizzy pop and test it each day by scratching it with a pin – you will find that the tooth gradually gets softer.

Healthy eating means variety, without eating too much. Have lots of fruit and vegetables – and a reasonable amount of meat. Eggs, milk and cheese will do instead of red meat or fish, if you are a vegetarian. Avoid too much fat, and don't eat between meals. Take time to chew and enjoy your food. Sensible eating and plenty of outdoor exercise should keep you alert and healthy.

Clean your teeth after breakfast and before bedtime.

Keeping warm and keeping cool

Taking your temperature

Winter or summer, your body keeps its temperature around 98.6° F – its "working temperature". Practice measuring temperature with the sort of thermometer used to show the temperature in houses. Measure how hot or cool it is in different parts of your home. "Cool" means "less hot". By the way, don't put one of these thermometers into boiling water!

To get a rough idea of your body temperature, tuck the thermometer inside your armpit for several minutes – and read it *at once* afterwards. Ask a doctor or a nurse to explain why they use a special thermometer to take your temperature *accurately*.

Energy from your food

Every time you move, your body burns a little fuel – glucose sugar (not quite the same as you put in tea), which is brought to muscles by your blood. If you don't overeat, most food you consume is converted into glucose, to provide energy to drive your "body machine". As you know, machines tend to get hot when they are working – and your body is no exception. The best way to keep warm in cold weather is to keep active. This can be your reward for shovelling snow!

What you sense as body heat is the vibration and shaking of all the billions of molecules in your body. Imagine the heat generated by dancers at a disco – and try to think of all those molecules as disco dancers. The *total* amount of movement is enormous, but each dancer only has a *share* of the energy. That share would be something like "temperature". Heat and temperature are different.

Put a peanut on a pin. Fix the pin in a blob of clay and place this on a saucer. When you set fire to the peanut, you get an impression of how much energy a peanut can supply as heat. **Be safe with matches and fire. Do this with an adult**.

Cool tips

Wet one hand with hot water. Hold both hands, side by side. The hot water evaporates (like sweat). Which hand feels cooler? Repeat, while making both hands equally more active – swing them to and fro.

These tests will help you to understand how sweating cools your skin. If you have a headache, lying down quietly with a folded wet flannel placed over your eyes will lessen the pain.

An old Chinese trick for keeping cool is to trickle very cold water over your wrists. Try it. Rubbing cold water over your face, using your hands, is an excellent way to "freshen up" in the morning!

Winter wisdom – projects to plan and do

1 Obtain several tins, all the same – lemonade cans will do. Also have ready pieces of different materials – such as cotton, fur, wool, kitchen foil. Fill the cans with hot water and "dress" each one in a different material. Which materials are best to stop heat escaping?

fill can with hot water
wrap with:
cotton
newspaper
wool
kitchen foil
etc!

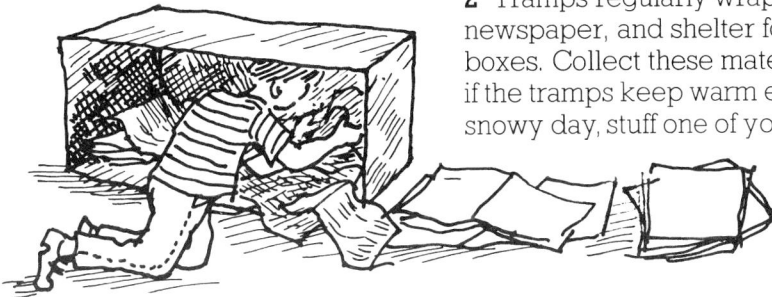

2 Tramps regularly wrap themselves in layers of newspaper, and shelter for the night in cardboard boxes. Collect these materials and do tests to find out if the tramps keep warm enough for comfort. On a snowy day, stuff one of your boots with newspaper.

3 If you use a hot-water bottle, wrap it in a sweater and rest it on your tummy – it warms you faster this way. **But don't use a hot-water bottle hot enough to burn you!** Ask a parent's advice. In wintry weather, wear several layers of clothes, including socks.

BODY MAGICAL CIRCUS – ACT 1

Lapping it up

SIT!

When a boy or a girl sits on your lap, you need a chair to support you – yet it is possible, without a single chair, for a hundred people to sit on one another's laps. They form a great circle, stand close to each other, and turn right. On a command of "Sit!", all sit down, on an endless chain of laps.

What a wonderful idea for a sponsored stunt. Imagine half the town's population sitting on each other's laps! French soldiers used to rest this way when marching over damp ground. But the Japanese hold the World Lap-Sitting Record.

PRESS HARD

A mind of its own

Stand sideways with your left (or right) side – foot, thigh, arm and shoulder – touching a wall. Press the outer part of your arm very hard against the wall. Keep pressing hard for about 20 seconds. Then move away. Much to your amazement, the arm seems to have a will of its own – it starts to rise in a magical way.

Heave Ho!

Sit in a straight-backed chair, with your back pressed against it and feet kept flat on the floor in front. Fold your arms. Now, without bending your back, try to stand. It's impossible. While you are sitting this way, the leg muscles are helpless – you need to lean forward, to put your body mass over your feet, but that's against the rules!

Getting a crush on you

Stand with arms out straight, with hands pressed flat against a wall. Challenge everybody in the room to act together and try to crush you. They must stand in line behind you, with arms outstretched and hands pushing on the shoulders of the person in front. You are the first in this line. Pretend to take the strain – but, in fact, each person's body takes only the force from the person immediately behind.

What can be held by your left but not by your right hand?

BODY MAGICAL CIRCUS - ACT 2

Thinking space

MANY VOLCANOES ERUPT MULBERRY JAM SANDWICHES UNDER NEGATIVE PRESSURE

The sentence above is nonsense, but well worth remembering. It could win you money on a TV quiz show. The first letters of each word are also the first letters of the names of the planets in the Solar System. They are in the correct order, going outwards from the sun. Can you tell me all the planets' names?

Number please

As quickly as possible and without reading the comments below, write the number twelve thousand, twelve hundred and twelve.

Challenge friends to do this in less than 7 seconds – after equipping them with pencils and papers. Do you all put "12 1212"? If so, try again by adding twelve thousand, twelve hundred and twelve.

You do some odd things when acting hastily.

Lost thumbs

Your hand, with its "controls" in your brain and nerves, is a marvellous machine – and its thumb is a superb feature of Nature's evolutionary design. No words can describe the value of a thumb so much as losing your use of it – temporarily, of course!

Tape together the thumb and first finger on each hand. Try to do your everyday activities, as usual. Thread a needle, unzip a banana, drink a mug of tea, comb your hair – you'll be grateful ever after for your wonderful thumbs.

Incredible duck-rabbit illusion

Ask a little child to tell you what
this is. (Make a copy of the
picture on a stiff card.)

Probable answer:
"A duck".

Then ask another child to say
what this is. (You have secretly
turned the card sideways.)

Probable answer:
"A rabbit".

sheet of
newspaper

Muscular hand ball

Hold the outside sheet of a newspaper – this will, in
fact, be four pages – in one hand. Can you crush the
paper into a tight paper ball?

You must use only one hand, and not rest the paper on
anything.

Children should try this with tabloid-size pages, but
adults must use full-size pages, such as *The New York
Times*. This game is excellent exercise for muscles in
the hand, **but please don't strain yourself**. This is
a great idea for party competitions.

Guessing what people will do

Put four shoeboxes in a row. Ask people to choose one. They must all look at the boxes from the same side of the table. Box **3**, counting from the left, is usually the most popular. Try this test on your class at school. You could hide a teddy in Box **3**. Then – if the test goes according to plan – you can show the teddy and the other empty boxes, to prove that you knew which box most of your helpers would choose.

Ask people to put cards colored bright yellow, blue, red and green, in order, with their favorite first and their most disliked color last. Test about 50 people, boys and girls about the same age. Which is the most liked and which the least liked color? Test another 50 people (perhaps children in another school). Results will probably be similar – but I can't be sure.

Most people do act in predictable ways much of the time. This means that you can be *fairly* certain about some of the things they do without thinking. If you are right-handed, you almost certainly put on your right glove first. People who want to sell you things study your habits, to try to make you buy without thinking – read on, to see what I mean.

The "mousetrap" on Main Street

There is a human mousetrap on Main Street of your town. It is the local supermarket. Has it got windows ablaze with FANTASTIC CUT-PRICE BARGAIN OFFERS? That is the "bait" for the tired, unsuspecting shopper – which could be you – who is the "mouse".

Inside the supermarket, do you hear soft, sweet music? That is to lull you into a happy buying mood. If you have an ordinary shopping-list, it will include: bread, cheese, toilet-rolls, vegetables, meat, beans, sugar and tea. These items are spread about all over the shop. Why don't the supermarket people make shopping easier by putting all these essential items in one place?

They want you to go into every part of the shop. They want you to see everything on display. They want to tempt you into buying more things than you really need. In a textbook written to teach supermarket managers, it says that customers are like mice, scurrying around the walls. The clever manager makes certain that the mouse – that's you – visits every part of the shop.

The things you need most are usually put low down on the shelves. This is to leave room at eye-level for expensive luxury items like tinned sweet-corn and game soup with sherry. But why are sweets put low enough for small children to see them?

Other "mousetrap" tricks include piling tins of soup into untidy heaps, where they look cheap, and putting SPECIAL OFFERS at corners, where they cannot be missed.

When the human mice reach the checking-out counter, where a smiling person waits, they could be caught again. There they discover "rewards", such as chocolate bars, crisps and glossy magazines. After all that hard work shopping, you deserve a reward! To be fair to the supermarket people, where else in town could you get so much for your money? If the supermarket did not sell so much and make so much money, the prices of the goods would be higher. Perhaps the "mice" do benefit. What do you think?

Preserve your memories

Make a careful record of a week's weather. The following week, ask young and old people if they can remember the weather on a certain day. You may be surprised at how untrustworthy memory is for this kind of detail. What did you have for dinner yesterday? Which way is Washington facing on a dollar bill? Is he facing the same way on a quarter? What color was the car parked near your school gate last Tuesday afternoon? (This might be an important clue for the police!)

Memory depends on interest and on your powers of observation – but, most importantly, it depends on how quickly you can find a particular "memory" when you need it. Sometimes you fail to come up with an answer to a quiz question, only to find that you knew it all along. You remembered the information, but were not able to re-call it from your brain.

apple	cheese
twins	mouse
story	tail
cheese	story
book	book
pear	leaf
tail	tree
leaf	apple
mouse	pear
tree	twins

Which of the lists do you remember in the shortest time? *Test yourself.* Notice how each word in one of the lists gives you a clue, to help you remember the next word. You remember things best when they make sense to you personally. Do you find you are a genius at remembering names of pop stars and sports players, but you find school subjects harder to remember? Sensible short sentences are easier than lists – try "Memory is being able to enjoy happy summer days in mid-winter".

Beware of gossip and rumors

Draw a simple picture of an unusual object. Show it to a friend for 5 seconds (just count five). Put the picture face down in a box. Your friend must draw a copy of the picture from memory and show it to another person for 5 seconds, before putting it in the box. Go on until about twenty people have helped. Then put the pictures, in the right order, in a line. Notice how the original idea has changed. This experiment shows how stories become changed through person-to-person gossip.

Improve your memory

"Richard Of York Gave Battle In Vain". Can you see the connection with the seven rainbow colors, in their correct order: Red, Orange, Yellow, Green, Blue, Indigo and Violet? Here is another one: "Tights come down!" Stalac*tites* come *down* from the ceilings of damp caves. Stalagmites grow up from the floor. These memory tricks are called mnemonics (pronounced without the first "m"). If you need to remember the five Great Lakes of North America, you will find the word HOMES useful – you may need to look in an atlas to see why.

Do you know Kim's Game, invented by the author of *The Jungle Book*? (Do you remember the author's name?) Put twenty objects on a tray and cover with a cloth. Uncover the objects for one minute and then ask your friends to write down as many as they can remember. Invent your own rules – make the game harder.

Keep a diary and take photographs for a family album. Both these are ways to boost your memory – you may have ambitions to be a writer. Your memory is the real you – the person you feel and know yourself to be. In the words of the Simon and Garfunkel song: "Preserve your memories – they're all that's left you".

Living in your world

Getting to know your neighborhood

Make a copy of this list and go for a walk in your neighborhood. Look for things described by words on the list – and write them down.

Find at least one of each, but more if you can. (Take a clip-board to rest your papers on.)

Beautiful	*Ugly*
High	*Low*
Sensible	*Foolish*
Happy	*Sad*
Shining	*Dull*
Hard	*Soft*
Soothing	*Frightening*
Huge	*Tiny*
Selfish	*Unselfish*
Funny	*Serious*
Old	*New*
Right	*Wrong*
I love	*I hate*
Friendly	*Unfriendly*
I can change	*I cannot change*

Your choices can be objects, people, animals, plants, living or dead, surfaces to touch, sounds, smells, personal feelings, etc.

Could you draw and color in a map of your neighborhood, showing a "trail" that others could use to find the things you found?

Trying to understand feelings

Look in a mirror. Try to be an actor or actress. Try to feel excited, then bored. It helps to imagine real exciting or boring things you know about. Let the feelings show in your face. Watch your eyes, eyebrows, cheeks, nose, mouth and chin – how do they change, to alter the expressions on your face?

Try other feelings: pleasure, joy, jealousy, anger, being frightened. Pretend to be confused – pretend your thoughts are mixed up and you feel lost. How does it look to be worried? Watch other people for expressions like these. Other people have feelings like yours. To be able to guess how other people might be feeling will help you to know and understand them better.

The secret of happiness

Do you expect people to be kind and caring? Perhaps you are lucky – you have friends, a cheerful family and other people who seem to know how you feel. I expect you are disappointed and lonely sometimes. Have you ever wondered: "Is there a secret of happiness?"

A wise person in China said that the main secret could be put into one word: *Shu*. It means "Do not do to others what you would not want done to yourself". Never expect to be thanked when you are kind and caring, but people often show they are grateful. Remember to say your own "thank yous". Your reward of happiness comes from good feelings in yourself – these come whenever you know that you have done your best.

Index